For Georgie
and Olivia

LITTLE TIGER PRESS
An imprint of Magi Publications
1 The Coda Centre, 189 Munster Road,
London SW6 6AW
www.littletigerpress.com
First published in Great Britain 2003
This edition published in 2008
Text and illustrations © Tim Warnes 2003
Tim Warnes has asserted his right
to be identified as the author and
illustrator of this work under the
Copyright, Designs and Patents Act, 1988.
Printed in China • All rights reserved
ISBN 978 1 84506 817 2
1 3 5 7 9 10 8 6 4 2

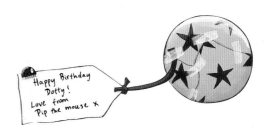

Happy Birthday
Dotty!
Love from
Pip the mouse X

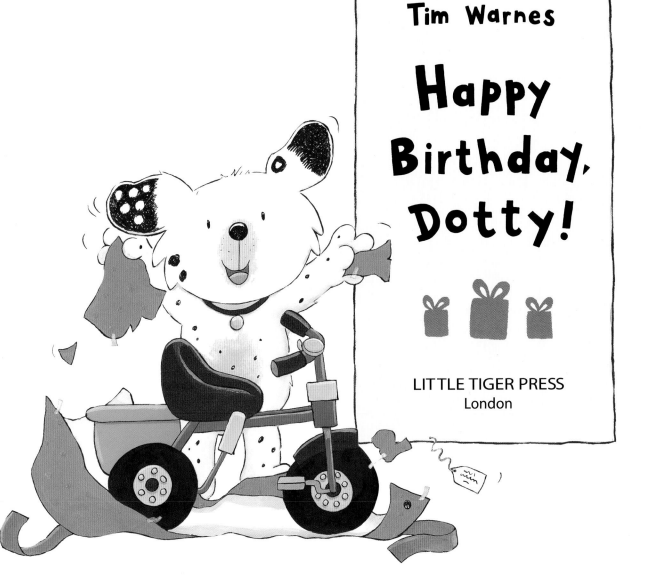

Tim Warnes

Happy Birthday, Dotty!

LITTLE TIGER PRESS
London

Dotty was very excited.
It was her birthday.

She had lots of cards
to open. But where were
all Dotty's friends?

Dotty went to find Pip the mouse.
Instead she found a little round
present with her name on it!

What could it be?

Happy Birthday
Dotty!
Love from
Pip the mouse x

Hooray!

A bouncy ball!

Happy Birthday
Dotty!
Love from
Pip the mouse X

As she chased after it,
Dotty spotted an arrow
on the floor. It pointed
to another and another.

It was a birthday trail!
Dotty followed the arrows . . .

. . . to the sandpit, where there was

another parcel. Dotty read the label.

"Happy Birthday, Dotty,

love from Tommy the tortoise."

What was it?

Delicious!

A yummy bone!

Dotty hurried across
the garden, following
the arrows to . . .

. . . Susie's apple tree.
Leaning against
her nest was
another present!

Yippee!

It was a kite from Susie!

But Susie wasn't there to help fly it.

Where was everyone?

Dotty was puzzled.
Taking all her presents,
she skipped along the trail
of arrows to . . .

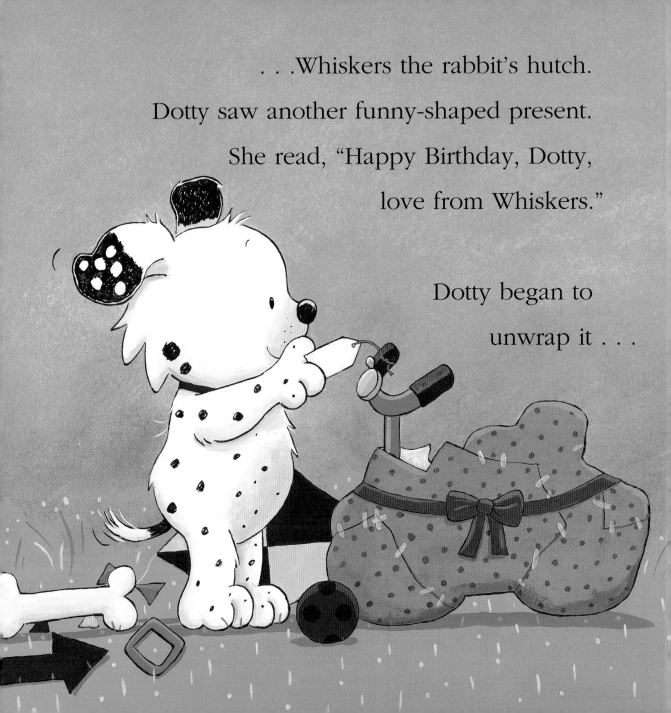

. . .Whiskers the rabbit's hutch.

Dotty saw another funny-shaped present.

She read, "Happy Birthday, Dotty,

love from Whiskers."

Dotty began to

unwrap it . . .

Wow!

A trike!

Dotty squealed with delight.
She popped all her
presents into the trailer.
She'd had lots of surprises,
but still Dotty's friends
were nowhere to
be seen.

Where could they be?
Maybe they had followed the
arrows too. Dotty climbed
on to her shiny new
trike and . . .

WHEEE!

She went to look for her friends.

Suddenly the trail ended.

Dotty was amazed to find . . .

. . . the

BIGGEST PRESENT

she had ever seen!

Dotty danced round
and round in circles.
What could this be?

"Surprise!
Happy Birthday, Dotty!"